First Edition
Paperback ISBN: 978-1-5324-2703-9
Hardcover ISBN: 978-1-5324-2704-6
eISBN: 978-1-5324-2702-2
Published in the United States by Xist Publishing
www.xistpublishing.com
PO Box 61593 Irvine, CA 92602

**Download a free eBook copy of this
book using this QR code.***

or at https://xist.pub/e66ab

* Limited time only
Your name and a valid email address are required to download.
Must be redeemed by persons over 13

Too School for Cool

{and other smarty-pants jokes}

Brenda Ponnay

xist Publishing

How do you make sure to get straight A's in school?

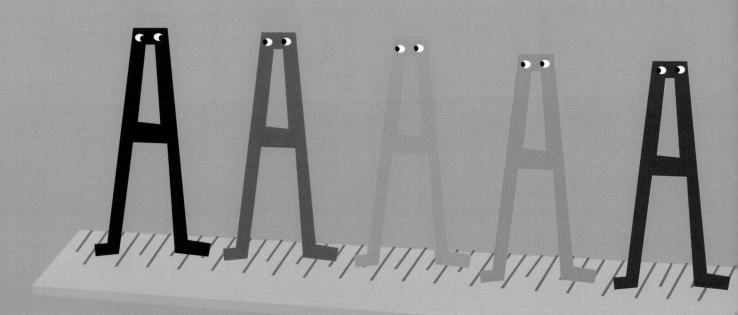

Use a ruler.

What did the pen say to the pencil?

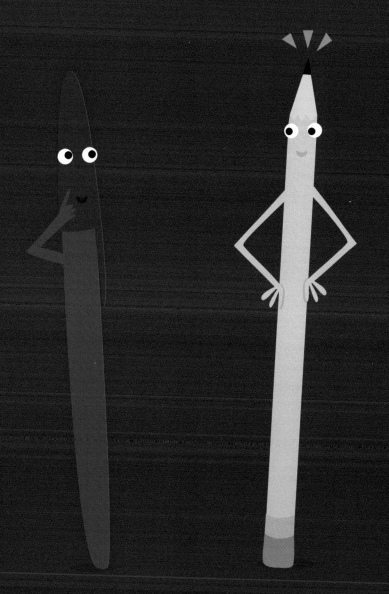

You have a point.

Why were the teacher's eyes crossed on the first day of school?

He couldn't control his pupils.

What flies around school at night?

An alphabat.

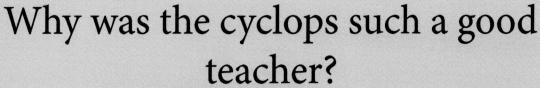

Why did the music teacher need a ladder?

To reach the really high notes.

Why was the backpack laying on the ground?

ZZZZZZZZZZZZZZZZZZZZZ

He was a napsack.

Why are geometry books so adorable?

They have acute angles.

Why did the girl
study in a tree?

She wanted a higher education.

What do elves study in school?

The Elfabet.

What do librarians take with them when they go fishing?

Bookworms!

Knock, knock.
Who's there?
Abby?
Abby who?

Abby C D E F G....

How do bees get to school?

On a School Buzz!

What kind of school do surfers go to?

Boarding school.

Why did two fours skip lunch?

They already 8.

What do you get if you add 2 oranges, 5 strawberries, 27 blueberries and one banana?

A delicious fruit salad!

Why did the teacher marry the janitor?

He swept her off her feet.

Why did the teacher write on the window?

She wanted her lessons to be perfectly clear.

About the Author

Brenda Ponnay is the author and illustrator of several children's books, including the popular Little Hoo series and several joke books. She lives in Southern California with her family.

Learn more about her Brenda and her books at brendaponnay.com

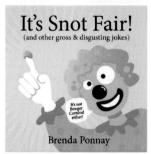 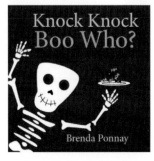 brendaponnay_books

Check out Brenda Ponnay's other joke books:

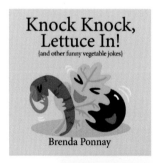

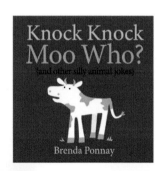

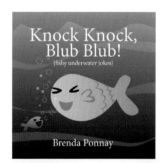

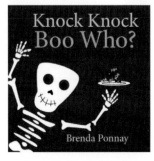

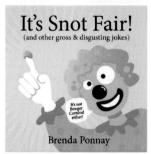